The Witch of Fourth Street

and Other Stories

THE WITCH OF FOURTH STREET

and Other Stories

by
MYRON LEVOY

Pictures by Gabriel Lisowski

HARPER & ROW, PUBLISHERS
New York, Evanston, San Francisco, London

Library of Congress Catalog Card Number: 74-183174

Trade Standard Book Number: 06-023795-3
Harpercrest Standard Book Number: 06-023796-1

For David and Debbie

Contents

The Witch of Fourth Street

and Other Stories

The Witch of Fourth Street

MANY years ago, a girl named Cathy Dunn came with her family from Dublin, Ireland, to the Lower East Side of New York. Everything in the new country fascinated her: fireworks and el trains and stickball games, and the songs of peddlers calling out their wares in a dozen languages. She loved to watch the policeman go by on his horse and the hook and ladder come round the corner like a long red dragon. But more than anything else, she loved to watch Mr. Coletti, the monkey man.

Mr. Coletti came to Second Avenue once or twice a week with his monkey, Espresso, and his hand organ, a big box on a wooden leg, which tweedled and tootled out a super-confabulation of sounds whenever he

1

turned the handle. He was an old, old man with white hair and a big white mustachio and eyes that crinkled up at the sides so that he always seemed to be laughing. And perhaps he always was, for the children of Second Avenue knew that Espresso was the funniest monkey in Manhattan.

Espresso would clap his hands and dance round and round in the circle formed by the children. When Mr. Coletti gave a little tug on the long yellow cord tied to the monkey's belt, Espresso would do a perfect somersault, sometimes two. If you held a penny out between your fingers, he would suddenly pluck it away and tip his little red cap. Then Mr. Coletti would say, "Hey, Espresso, give the penny to the boss, huh? Put her in the bank." And Espresso would drop the penny into Mr. Coletti's pocket while the children cheered. And Espresso could ride a tiny tricycle and make the funniest faces and . . . what's the use. You had to see him to believe it.

Often, at home, Mr. Coletti would scold Espresso— in Italian, because Espresso didn't understand very much English. "Hey, *bambino,* why do you make so many faces, huh? I didn't teach you to make dopey faces, bambino." And his wife would smile as she drank her coffee, for Mr. Coletti called her *bambina,* even though she was seventy-three. Mr. Coletti called

2

every old person bambina or bambino, little girl or little boy, and he called every child under ten *signore* or *signora,* sir or madam. It seemed to make everyone happy.

Of all the children who loved Espresso, Cathy Dunn loved him the most. Cathy was given a penny a day for candy, but she always saved those pennies for Espresso. She would rather see Espresso tip his hat to her than have the three vanilla cookies or the two braids of licorice a penny could buy in those days.

But Cathy was just a little frightened of Espresso, not because he was a monkey, but because on certain days Cathy was convinced that he *wasn't* a monkey. When he blinked his eyes so mischievously and did such human tricks, Cathy would be reminded of stories she'd heard back in Ireland about the little people—the elves and leprechauns. It seemed perfectly obvious to her: Espresso was a leprechaun. It was a delicious secret. Only she and Espresso knew it. Espresso would blink at her and she would blink back in their private leprechaun language.

One day, Cathy was standing in the circle of children watching Espresso. She held her penny tightly in her fingers as if it were about to fly like a bird from its nest. She was waiting, waiting for the right moment to hand it to Espresso.

4

But the monkey just didn't seem to notice Cathy's penny. "Hey, looka there, the little signora," said Mr. Coletti. But no, Espresso was too busy having an ugly-face contest with Joey Basuto.

Then Aaron Kandel, who lived next door, said to Cathy, "You got to hold it by the rim. Otherwise he won't take it."

"He *knows* me," said Cathy. "He *always* takes it. Let's see *you* do it!"

"Naa, not me," said Aaron. "I always save my pennies for the witch."

The witch? That was even better than a leprechaun. Cathy was about to ask *which* witch, but realized how silly that would sound and asked, *"What* witch?"

"The witch!" said Aaron. "The witch! You know! The *witch!*"

"I don't know about any witch," said Cathy. "Which witch do you mean?"

"Come on, I'll show you," Aaron said.

Cathy had never seen a witch, not even back in Ireland where children often saw witches hiding in the early morning mists and in the evening shadows. And though she was afraid of witches, Cathy had always wanted to see one. From a distance, naturally.

They walked along Fourth Street toward the school. Cathy walked that way every day, yet she'd never

5

noticed a witch. Was Aaron trying to play a joke on her? He probably was. He liked to play jokes on all the girls, and particularly the ones who giggled a lot.

"There!" Aaron was pointing up the block, toward an old lady seated on a wooden crate. "That's her," he whispered. It was the pencil lady.

"Is she a *witch*?" asked Cathy.

"Of course she is," whispered Aaron. "And you'd better make sure you give her a penny every day. Or *else*!"

Yes. It was so obvious if you really looked. The old woman was dressed all in black, her face was wrinkled, her hands were twisted like roots torn from the earth. In her lap was an open box of pencils and a tin tray holding a few pennies. Her head was down; she looked at nothing.

"She can see *everything*," whispered Aaron. "She's a witch!"

Cathy shuddered. Her heart felt like a big bass drum being pounded in a parade. She was very frightened, but strangely happy. She couldn't believe her luck! She'd been walking right past a live witch on the way home from school every single day! Look at her! Oh, what an evil woman! It was wonderful! Now she had a witch as well as a leprechaun.

"Give her your penny," whispered Aaron, "or

she'll turn you into a stick or a spider. She's got all kinds of witch spells."

The penny felt warm, almost alive, in Cathy's fingers. She took a deep breath, said a quick prayer, crossed herself twice, then dashed forward, dropped the penny into the tray, sprang back, and ran. When she turned back to look, the woman's head was nodding up and down as if she were thanking someone . . . or saying yes to the devil.

That next Monday on the way home from school, Cathy dropped another penny into the old woman's lap. And by Wednesday she'd even found the courage to take a pencil, though she threw it away a moment later, for she feared it might be a snake or an eel turned into a pencil by the witch's magic. And the woman's head went up and down, up and down. The witch was satisfied.

But on Thursday, as Cathy started home from school, she heard familiar music wheedling and yodeling from the direction of Second Avenue. It was Espresso and the monkey man! She hadn't seen them for a week.

Cathy started to run, her schoolbag bumping up and down in her hand. Perhaps if she ran past the witch fast enough, the witch wouldn't notice her. She tried to look straight ahead, very politely, as if she'd simply forgotten that the witch was there. But she couldn't help seeing the witch out of the corner of her eye, sitting like a huge raven tucked in its feathers.

In that brief glimpse, Cathy saw that the witch was looking directly at her. Eyes blacker than obsidian. It was too late! Cathy had not given the witch her penny. And the witch had cast her spell.

Cathy ran as fast as she could, not to the monkey man, but straight home. In her bedroom, she prayed trembling on her bed, but she didn't quite know why she prayed. God certainly didn't believe in witches.

"Don't let me die! Don't let me turn into a spider or a toad! Please! Make her forget about me! Make her not know my name! Please!"

That evening Cathy came down with a fever. She shivered and sweated and shivered again. Clearly, the witch was working her magic in her. Cathy knew it was only a matter of time before her mother would come into the room and see a lizard or a goat tucked under the blankets. And if she were turned into a spider, her mother might never find her. The horrible thought crossed Cathy's mind: she might even step on me!

While her mother rubbed her arms and legs with cold wet towels, Cathy pleaded ferverishly, "It's the witch. I didn't give her my penny. Please, Mommy, give her my penny. Give her my penny."

Mrs. Dunn tried to soothe Cathy. "Now, now, now, now *macushla,* m'darling, you're all full of the old fairy tales again. You're in a fever, that's what 'tis. There's no witches, m'little sick darling, not a one in the whole world."

"Yes, there is! She's got me in her spell! She's the witch of Fourth Street! Ask Aaron Kandel. Give her my penny! Please! *Mommy, please!*"

Mrs. Dunn sent her son, Neil, for Dr. Belasco. The doctor came in, huffing and puffing from the four flights of stairs. He examined Cathy carefully, going *hmm humm* every few moments. He examined her ears, *hmm,* eyes, *ahum,* throat, *hmm hmm,* nose, *aha,* chest, *humm,* and stomach, *hmm humm hmm.* Then he frowned.

"*Humm.* An infection," he said. "No other symptoms. *Hmm* . . . plenty of liquids. Lots of rest. Cold rubdowns. I see you've done that, very good. Two aspirins every . . . *humm, hmm,* make it four hours. Let me know how she is tomorrow. Has to run its course . . . *ahum. Ahem.* Yes. That will be two dollars, house call. Much obliged. Don't worry. Has to run its course."

But the next morning Cathy was still feverish. She knew it was the witch, but her mother just didn't want

9

to understand. "Please, Mommy, take my penny to the witch. You've got to!"

"Hush, hush, macushla, 'tis your fever talking," Mrs. Dunn said softly.

But finally, Mrs. Dunn decided to take the penny to the old woman just to ease Cathy's mind. Whoever she was, she shouldn't be allowed in the street, scaring little children like that.

But when Mrs. Dunn saw the old woman on Fourth Street sitting quietly on her wooden crate, she knew that it was just a poor old woman selling pencils. Though she had to admit the old woman did look a little frightening. And when she dropped Cathy's penny in the tray, Mrs. Dunn couldn't help feeling a slight shiver. Oh, we Dunns have too much imagination, she thought. 'Tis a curse and a blessing at once.

When she told Cathy that the penny had been delivered, Cathy seemed to relax for the first time since she'd come home the day before. She had tossed feverishly all night, but now she turned over and slept for three hours. And when she awoke, the fever had broken.

"Mommy, I'm hungry," she called from the bedroom. "Can I have hash and eggs and toast with jelly on it and also butter but mostly jelly and some milk?" And Mrs. Dunn knew that Cathy was going to be well.

From that day on, Cathy walked two blocks out of her way, one downtown to Third Street and one back up, to avoid passing the witch. She saved her pennies for the monkey man and for lollipops large as moons, and swore she would never go past the witch again. For the witch was an evil, ugly witch who cast spells on children, even though they'd given her penny after penny after penny.

The days grew shorter, and the monkey man came earlier and left earlier, as soon as dusk fell. And one late afternoon in November, Cathy and her friend Noreen decided to follow the monkey man to see what he did with the monkey.

"I'll bet he drops him off at the pet shop every night," said Noreen.

"No," said Cathy, "I'll bet the monkey turns into a little man, like a dwarf, and goes around repairing things in houses and stores. And people leave him presents."

"Let's see," said Noreen.

Mr. Coletti slid the heavy barrel organ to his side. Then, tilted way over for balance, and with Espresso perched on one shoulder, the monkey man walked slowly away. Cathy and Noreen followed, waving at the monkey whenever he blinked at them.

Then Cathy's heart froze. They were going along

Fourth Street, heading right toward the witch! Yes, there she was, sitting on her crate with her pencils and her tin tray.

As the monkey man walked toward her, Espresso suddenly started to twitter and jump up and down. Espresso could tell she was a witch! Any leprechaun could. And the witch turned and looked up. She was going to put a spell on the monkey man! Cathy wanted to shout, but she was afraid the witch would look at her and turn her to ashes on the spot.

And then . . . it couldn't be! The monkey man bent over and *kissed* the witch on her cheek! And the witch stood up and poured the pennies from her tray into the monkey man's pocket. Then she kissed him *and* the monkey, and gave the monkey some nuts to eat from her hand. How could she be a witch and do that?

The monkey man and his wife walked off together, laughing and talking in Italian, while Espresso happily jumped back and forth from one shoulder to the other. They turned in at an old brownstone building, and together lifted the organ up the high row of front steps. Soon, a light went on at a second-floor window and Espresso, without his cap and jacket, leaped to the windowsill, a plain, ordinary monkey.

12

He looked out, blinked at the children, then jumped back into the room.

Cathy and Noreen laughed and turned to go home. Witches indeed! Leprechauns indeed! Her mother had been right. There were no witches, not a one in the whole world.

But as they walked home, Cathy felt a sadness creep over her, like the fog that used to creep over the streets beyond her bedroom window when she had been a very little girl back in Dublin, Ireland, and had really believed in witches and the little people and fairies and dragons and all sorts of terrible, frightening, wonderful things.

Vincent-the-Good
and the Electric Train

THERE once was a boy who lived in an old, crowded tenement near Second Avenue. He was so generous and good that everyone believed he might grow up to become a saint, in the same way that some boys grew up to become firemen or baseball champions. His name was Vincent DeMarco, and he had no brothers or sisters or anyone but his father and mother.

He was not an unusually good student in school and was certainly not a good stoopball player nor a good roller skater. He was just good.

If he had been only somewhat good or pretty good or fairly good, he would probably have been called a sissy by the other boys on his block. But he was so

14

good that he was called Vincent-the-Good with a certain awe and respect.

When someone asked him for a piece of candy, he gave two pieces. When his parents took him to church, he put all his savings, his pennies and nickels, into the poor box. And he always helped the smaller boys when they were being bullied. Even his mother and father were a little awed by a boy who was that good.

At first, the other boys tried to make him do something wrong, but it was no use. Vincent could no more do wrong than stop breathing. The priest, Father O'Connell, was convinced that Vincent, in some way, had been singled out by God for "great things as yet unknown."

Great things as yet unknown! The sweet words, the beautiful words, filled Mr. and Mrs. DeMarco with wonder. God had blessed them with an overwhelming gift. And yet . . . how hard it was to have a son who was not really like other boys. And secretly, though they wouldn't admit it to each other, they wished that Vincent would perhaps do something just a little bit, a tiny, tiny bit wrong, even if it meant he would not be a saint.

It would soon be Vincent's eleventh birthday. Birthday parties were rare treats in those days because parties cost money and everyone was poor. Russian,

Polish, Irish, Italian, Hungarian, German, Protestant, Catholic, Jewish, everyone was a brother in one way, surely: everyone was poor. But Mr. and Mrs. DeMarco had decided that Vincent would have a birthday party. A boy that good, a boy who was destined for great things as yet unknown, such a boy must have at least one real birthday party. And not only a birthday party, but a stupendous present. What would it be?

Mr. DeMarco worked in a change booth at one of the stations on the Second Avenue elevated train line, which everyone called the Second Avenue el. He sat behind a window that was protected by iron bars, except for a little opening above a wooden counter. All day long, people pushed dimes and quarters and half dollars in through the opening, and he pushed nickels for the turnstile back out to them. While the trains squealed and screeched in and out of the station, Mr. DeMarco made change. A quarter in, five nickels out: zip, zip, zip, zip, zip. Half dollar in, a quarter *and* five nickels out: ZIP, zip, zip, zip, zip, zip.

But while he made change, his hands flying like a surgeon's, Mr. DeMarco daydreamed of the trains and imagined himself as the motorman, up front. The joy of it: to ease into the station, past the waiting crowd, right up to the far end with the first car. Then, stop. The conductors on each car opening the gates. The passengers getting off and on. Everyone aware of that man up front, with the power of electric motion in his hands. The passengers sitting in the cross-seats or facing-seats or standing, holding on to straps during the crowded rush hour. Then the conductors slamming the gates shut and pulling on the bell cords, in order, from the rear of the train to the front, car by car: ding-ding . . . ding-ding . . . ding-ding . . . ding-ding . . . ding-ding. All clear. Ready to go. The train hiccuping, jolting, and then moving slowly, smoothly, *yaaa-yeaaaaa-ahhhh,* out of the station. Yes! Definitely! *Sì. Definitivamente.* The present would be an electric train set. *Un treno elèttrico.*

But an electric train set on Second Avenue! Why, one could scarcely earn enough for milk and bread and rent and shoes. How could anyone afford an electric train, a real Lionel train? By putting pieces of cardboard inside his shoes to cover the holes. By patching the patches on his coat. By not eating very much. And on some days, not eating at all.

And so Vincent's birthday came, a Saturday in fall, as bright and blue as the flight of a jay. The train set, wrapped in yellow paper with a red string, lay hidden under the big bed. Every half hour, Mr. DeMarco went into the bedroom to make sure the box hadn't disappeared.

The ice cream. The cake. Laughter, games, noise. And then, time for the present. Mr. DeMarco brought the great yellow package into the room amid a sudden hush. While every boy stared, the wrappings came off, the box was opened, and there, nested in separate little compartments, were a perfect miniature engine and coal tender and five orange, red, green, yellow, blue freight cars. And tracks. Curved. Straight. A station. A semaphore pole. A switch. A control box. Everything.

The boys whistled softly, and one said, "You're lucky, Vince." And another said, " I wish I was you, Vince."

Patiently, carefully, Mr. DeMarco assembled the tracks and connected the wires and put the cars delicately in place, checking that each wheel was properly on the rail.

Power on. Slowly, majestically, the train left the station. Round the first turn. More power. Highballing to the second turn. Ease off. Round the second turn. Back to the station. To the far end of the station. Easy. Easy. Stop.

Mrs. DeMarco suggested that Mr. DeMarco let

Vince try it. And that every boy be given a turn.

Yes. Good. But carefully, carefully. Mr. DeMarco stayed near the controls, watching, his hand in the air right above the hand of the boy operating the train. Steady! Easy!

Two hours passed so quickly that they seemed a minute and a half. It was almost time for the boys to go home. So Mr. DeMarco took the set apart and placed each car and track back in the cutouts and compartments in the box, as carefully as if he were decorating a Christmas tree. The boys lingered, watching each detail of the ceremony. Then Mr. DeMarco went into the bedroom and lay on the bed, arms under his head, happy that he was in America at a time when such marvels could be bought for an eleven-year-old boy.

In the living room, the boys stood staring at the box, unable to go, unable to turn away from such perfection.

"Hey, I wish your father was my father, Vince," one boy said.

"You're lucky. I'd give my right arm for a train," said another.

"He got it 'cause he's good," said a third.

And suddenly, Vincent felt his heart twist in him

and fall, like a kite tangled in its tail. He took the engine out of its compartment in the box and thrust it into a boy's hands. And the gondola car. And the yellow box car. The flat car. The tank car. The red caboose. The station. The semaphore pole. The tracks.

Mrs. DeMarco, coming in from the kitchen with a *caramella* candy for each boy to take home, saw Vincent give the last of the tracks away. She cried out, "*Lunàtico!* What are you doing? What are you *doing*?"

"Go on home!" Vincent called to the boys. "Take the trains and go home."

Vincent's father, hearing the commotion, jumped off the bed, his suspenders hanging at his sides, and hurried to the living room. But it was too late. As the last of the boys raced out the door and down the stairs, Mr. DeMarco shouted, his voice echoing in the tiled hallway, "Come back! Come back! *Ladri!* Thieves! Come back!"

Then he returned to the living room, fell into a chair and let his head sink down on the table. All those months, hungry half the day and every night. To save. For what! For *this*? That beautiful chain of cars, the little wheels that clicked over the rails like those on a real train, the tiny light in front of the engine, the perfect harmony of the busy drive rods were gone, all gone. How bitter it was to have a son like this.

Vincent's mother stared at the box on the floor. Empty. The whole house seemed empty. She spoke, not to Vincent but to herself, *"Vincenzo, Vincenzo, strambo ragazzo,* strange boy, what have you done to us?"* Great things as yet unknown? Perhaps. But how bitter it was to have a son like this.

The box on the floor was empty. Mr. DeMarco felt it as an emptiness in his own body. He couldn't raise his head from the table. God had given him a saint for a son, but how bitter it was.

Vincent heard his father moaning to himself. "My train. He gave my train away. Just like *that.* Here. Take it . . ."

My train? Vincent felt angry. Fair is fair! Wasn't it supposed to be his, *Vincent's,* train to do with as he wished? *Wasn't it?* But then Vincent thought of how his father had wanted to play with the train even more than his friends. Of course! His father *loved* the train. It had been a present for Vincent, but it had also been a present for his father. He'd had no right to give it away!

He must get the train back. But how? He could just ask his friends to give it back, but he knew they wouldn't. When they found something in the street, a lost penknife or a cap gun, they would never look for the owner as Vincent did. They were too poor, too starved for toys. Finders keepers, losers weepers. Why, then, should they return something *given* to them?

Still, he would try. And if they didn't return it? For the first time in his life, Vincent decided to do something bad. If a boy didn't return the train, he would tell the boy's mother that he had stolen it at the birthday party. Had stolen a car, a track, a semaphore pole. Then he would *have* to give it back. Yes, Vincent would lie for the sake of his father.

But all this would have to wait until tomorrow; it was time for bed. It meant he would have to lie on Sunday, of all days.

Under the covers, Vincent curled up into a tight ball and hoped he could fall asleep without thinking. He shut his eyes, but his mind raced round and round a track, just like his electric train. No one would ever call him Vincent-the-Good again. Vincent-the-Bad would be his new name. There goes Vincent-the-Bad! Look at him! Round and round went Vincent's thoughts. Would his father put his head down on his arms again, when he'd learned Vincent had lied? And would his mother wring her hands and call him: *"Bugiardo!* Liar!"?

Vincent-the-Bad. He felt almost relieved; he had been Vincent-the-Good for too long. So be it. Vincent-the-Good was dead. There goes Vincent-the-Bad! Look! He saw himself, his mouth twisted from the lies, his tongue burning as from hot soup. Do not speak to him! Liar! . . . No! No! It was ugly! He didn't want to be Vincent-the-Bad! But he must get those trains back! He *must*!

Confused and troubled, Vincent prayed that God would not punish him too harshly for the crime to come. Then he turned over and let his tightly curled body open up like a flower, and he fell asleep.

Church was difficult for Vincent that Sunday morning. All night he had dreamed that Father O'Connell was giving a sermon on lying. But when the sermon came, Vincent sighed with relief: it was on the need for a new hospital. Afterward, Vincent put a bright new nickel, with the face of an Indian on one side and a buffalo on the other, into the box for hospital donations. But his heart was knocking inside him, for soon it would be time to get the train.

When he reached home, Vincent went into the bedroom and put on his worn pants and old sweater. He must not tell those lies in his good Sunday clothes; that would be honoring the crime. Then he walked into the kitchen and told his mother he was going out to play stickball. The first lie! His face flushed.

He went to Frank Milano's apartment first, on Third Avenue. But Frank wasn't home; he had gone out somewhere, for something. All right, he'd try again later. Then he went over to Timmy McCarthy's, but Timmy was out, too. And Joey Basuto. Out. Everybody was out. Were they hiding from him?

Vincent walked home slowly, past a patchwork of smells from all the Sunday dinners being prepared in the tenements along the way: lasagna, chicken *paprikasch*, corned beef and cabbage, goulash, sauerkraut, *kielbasa*, *piroshki*. And the breads and rolls and cakes baking and the soups simmering. Though everyone was poor, on Sunday everyone managed to have something special, a favorite dish, a prized dessert. But Vincent didn't find his mouth watering as it usually did on Sundays at one o'clock. There would be no joy in any meal for him until he'd gotten the train back.

Vincent climbed the flights of stairs up to the third floor. The hallway had been invaded by the smell of his mother's very special and secret meat sauce, a sauce and smell different from any other on the East Side, or in New York, or in the entire United States. Mrs. Dunn's Irish stew with its nice, delicate aroma of potatoes and lamb couldn't compete at all, and the smell of Mrs. Kandel's strudel next door, though fresh and sweet, fell to the ground, dead, at the very sound of his mother's spoon stirring the magic mixture. A victorious sauce; his favorite smell and taste in the world. But today, Vincent scarcely noticed the smell at all.

He put his hand on the doorknob, but didn't turn it. What was *this*? From within, he heard his father singing an aria from *La Bohème: "Che gelida manina, se la lasci riscaldar. . . ."* Your tiny hand is frozen, let me warm it for you. . . . *And* his mother was humming along with him! Wait, wait! There was something else! The sound of a clicketa-clicketa-clicketa-clicketa-clicketa. The train! It was the train!

Vincent burst into the living room and stood there, astounded. For there was Frank Milano operating a switch. And Joey Basuto at the control box, and Timmy McCarthy preparing a pile of little wooden matches, as logs for hauling on the flat car. And Vito and Jack and Nicholas. Everything was back in place around the track, even the little man on the station holding a red flag. And his father had his hand near the controls again, ready for any emergency. A miracle!

Timmy spoke first. "What's the matter, Vince?

Why you standing there? I couldn't do nothing with just a control box and no trains. I went over to Joey's to get the engine, that's all."

Then Joey said, "Sure, but what good is it without tracks? We got the tracks back from Frank, except that Vito had six curved ones. He didn't wanna give 'em up, neither, huh, Vito? Stingy!"

"I did *so*! It was the gondola and the flat car I didn't want to give back."

"So we figured it's no good like this. All we'd do is fight," said Joey. "So we brought it back. It's yours anyhow. Your father said we could come over and play with it though."

"Yeah," said Vito. "You better listen to your father, or else. Right, Mr. DeMarco?"

"He'll listen," said Nicholas. "He's good old Vincent-the-Good."

Vincent-the-Good, who had almost become Vincent-the-Bad, knelt by the tracks and watched the locomotive pull five times its weight. Clicketa-clicketa-clicketa clicketa-clicketa. He looked across at his father who was laughing and singing, and for the first time that day he felt hungry.

Round and round the train went, hauling its freight to Detroit and Chicago and St. Louis. Hauling matchsticks and paper clips and logs and iron ingots and cattle and coal and oil. The click of the train and his father's voice became one song, a duet in praise of machinery and electricity and power and movement and America. But to Vincent, it had become a song in praise of God.

Andreas and the Magic Bells

IF you had lived on the East Side of New York many years ago, you might have awakened to the cry of *"Yaa!* Old clothes! *Yaaa!"* And if you had looked out the window and down the street you would undoubtedly have seen Andreas Kastanakis on his old, old wagon pulled by his old, old horse. And in the wagon, piled high, you would have seen used clothes that Andreas bought and then resold to others.

The wagon rattled and daddled and squeaked and squawked along, while up front, a string of iron cowbells clinked and clunked and glinked, endlessly. And the old horse's hooves made a slow clap . . . clop on the cobbles. And so you would have heard: *"Yaa!* Old clothes!" Clink-clunk, clap . . . clop,

clinkety-clunk, clap . . . clop . . . clap . . . clop.
"*Yaa!* Old clothes!" Clink-clunk, clap . . . clop
. . . clap . . . clop.

Andreas had named his horse Socrates after a
famous philosopher of ancient Greece, because the
horse always looked so sad and serious, as if he were
trying to decide the reason why horses have four legs
while old-clothes men have only two legs. Socrates
was almost twenty years old, which meant he was
about as old as a man of sixty or seventy. And lately,
Andreas had noticed that the brisk clip-clop-clip-clop
of earlier days had changed to that slow clap . . .
clop . . . clap . . . clop. To make matters worse,
Socrates' head hung lower and lower as time went by,
until the poor horse seemed to be counting the cobblestones as he walked. Andreas was very worried, for he
was afraid that Socrates was at the end of his days.

Andreas himself was a sight to behold. He wore
a rather battered top hat, a pair of white gloves which
were missing their white thumbs, a wool sweater that
had managed to entertain a family of moths one long,
pleasant winter and now had as many holes as a honey-
comb, a pair of trousers which shone at the knees like
the halves of two bowling balls, and shoes that were
slightly unusual in that the right shoe was brown and
the left was black. Ah, but they fitted his feet beauti-

fully. Andreas' right foot was somehow larger than his left, and he had searched through all his merchandise for a proper match. But to balance the shoes, Andreas wore a black sock on his right foot and a brown on his left.

Andreas sold the best of the old clothes to the poor people along his route. The rest were sold by the batch to be processed into paper, or shredded and stuffed into sofas and mattresses. Sometimes a house-wife would sell Andreas a used coat or dress and then buy a different one from off his wagon, and in this way she could get a change of outfit for pennies. And when this happened, Andreas would always say, "Ah, it becomes you beautiful, madam. Now you look like a queen, while before you only looked like a princess." And Socrates would nod his head as if to say *yea,* instead of the *neighhh* which actually came out.

Clap . . . clop . . . clap . . . clop . . . clap . . . clop went old Socrates along Fourth Street. *"Gee-yap!"* called Andreas. *"Gee-yap!"* But he knew it was useless. Socrates no longer seemed to care; the horse simply clap . . . clopped along as people breathe, unthinkingly, in order to stay alive.

Ah, well, thought Andreas, it's time I took Socrates to Dr. Withers. His eyes have looked pink lately, which is nice for a white rabbit, but bad for a brown

31

horse. And so Andreas unhitched Socrates from the wagon and led him toward the East River where Dr. Withers, the horse specialist, had his office in an old trolley barn.

When Andreas arrived with Socrates, Dr. Withers was rushing about in the dark barn, busily swatting horseflies with a rolled-up copy of the *Veterinarian's Journal.* "Got you, you crazy devil!" he shouted at a fly that buzzed away out of reach.

Then he saw Andreas and Socrates. "Ah, patients, patients," he said. "What seems to be the trouble? Touch of the strangles? Bit of shipping fever? Pinworms? Roundworms? Botflies? Lice? Mange? Ticks? You name it, we'll cure it. That horse doesn't look good. Not good. Let me have a look at him. Bring him around over to here."

Dr. Withers examined Socrates' forehead, eyes, nostrils, muzzle, teeth, throat, crest, and poll. Then he checked the horse's flanks, hocks, fetlocks, gaskins, pasterns, and hooves, and, yes, his withers. Then he turned to Andreas, wiped the sweat from his brow, and said, "Very simple. The horse is old. To most people with a horse like that, I'd say: have him destroyed. Put him out of his misery. Just like that. But I can see you love that horse. I can always tell. It's the way you walked in here, kind of slow, and the way he followed you. Trust. Faith. Love. Care. Comradeship. Affection. Loyalty. Mutual respect. I can always tell. So . . . in *your* case, I say feed him proper—it's all in the feed. Reduce the hay, add more oats—are you writing this down?—check for mold in the grain, lace it with wheat bran or soybean meal, try a touch of barley, and make sure you stick to alfalfa at all costs. You do that, and he's bound to pick up. I know my horses. Look out! There's a big green fly on your hat!"

And down came the folded-up *Veterinarian's Journal* right on Andreas' top hat. "Got you, you crazy devil!" shouted Dr. Withers.

The fly escaped, as usual, but the hat did not. It folded on Andreas' head like an accordion.

Andreas was about to protest, but he'd learned over the years that it rarely paid to protest to officials of any sort. And Dr. Withers, being a doctor, was almost the same as an official.

In the days that followed, Andreas reduced the hay in Socrates' feed, and added more oats and wheat bran and a touch of barley, and stuck to alfalfa at all costs, just as Dr. Withers had advised. But Socrates still clap . . . clopped through the streets as slowly as ever, with his head down.

Ah me, thought Andreas. It hasn't helped. That doctor isn't any better at curing horses than he is at killing flies. Perhaps Socrates needs a new bit. He seems to be pulling and nagging at this one. I'll go to the harness maker.

The walls of the harness maker's shop were covered with saddles, and hanging down from hooks in the ceiling, bridles and straps and stirrups and reins touched one another, thick as vines in a jungle. The whole shop smelled of oil and leather, and to those who loved horses it was sweeter than perfume.

The harness maker examined Socrates' harness carefully, particularly the cheek straps and noseband and bit and throatlatch. Then he said, "*Hmm.* Nothing wrong with that harness. That harness is a good harness. Trouble is, the horse has no spirit. Better have him shot before he falls in the street. Like to sell you a new harness, mister, but what you need's a new horse."

Poor Andreas. As he left the harness maker's shop, his head was as low as Socrates'. And the bells on the wagon, clinking and clunking, seemed to have their heads low, too. Old age was old age. How could you cure old age? For eighteen years, Socrates and Andreas had worked together on the streets of the Lower East Side. Socrates had been Andreas' first friend in America. When Andreas had arrived from Greece with just enough money for a horse and wagon, he had picked out Socrates from all the other horses because he had looked so sad and noble. But now Socrates only looked sad.

"Ah, ah, ah!" called Andreas' friend, Mario Basuto, the vegetable man, as their wagons drew together along Second Avenue. "What's the matter, hey? You look like the world is finished."

"Socrates is finished," answered Andreas.

"What do you mean!" shouted Mario, as an el train roared by overhead. "You got plenty of horse there. Plenty of horse."

"Old age!" called Andreas. "My horse is dying of old age. Don't get too close. He may fall on your wagon."

"You don't take care of him," called Mario. "That's all it is. Look at *my* horse. He's old, too. But my boy, Joey, he combs and curries him every day. Makes the horse feel younger. And I put flowers in his mane. I clip his tail. And then the ladies know that my vegetables must be good. If my horse is fresh and clean, how can my tomatoes be bad? If my horse feels young at heart, how can my cantaloupes be rotten?" And with that, Mario turned his horse and wagon onto Sixth Street.

Maybe Mario is right, thought Andreas. Maybe Socrates doesn't feel young at heart. It's all in how you feel. I'll follow Mario's advice.

All that next Sunday, Andreas worked on Socrates, fixing and fussing and brushing and combing. And on Monday he set out along his usual route, shouting his usual shout: *"Yaa!* Old clothes! *Yaaa!"* But the wagon still rattled and daddled and squeaked and squawked and the bells up front still clinked and clunked and glinked. And Socrates, curried, combed, and covered with flowers, still clap . . . clop . . . clap . . . clopped along, slower and sadder than ever. If anything, the flowers seemed to weigh him down further, as if they were the very last straw to his burden of years.

"It's no use!" called Andreas, out loud. "No use! My horse is finished! Finished! It's no use!"

At that moment, Andreas' wagon happened to be passing in front of a small dark shop on Second Avenue. The sign above the door read: Petrescu's Antiques. And from somewhere within, the vague tinkling sound of bells reached the street, then faded away.

An ordinary enough event, except that for the few seconds that the bells tinkled, Socrates raised his head high! And when the bells stopped, his head drooped again. Then the bells sounded for another second, and again Socrates raised his head!

"Astounding!" said Andreas. "Miraculous! *Those* are the bells I need for my wagon! Not these miserable iron bells that glunk and clunk. I must have those bells!" And Andreas pulled the wagon over to the curb and rushed into the dark, dusty shop.

Petrescu, the owner, was sitting in his chair thinking of his childhood in Rumania. He thought of the river that flowed through the middle of the town of Oradea where he was born, and the bridges and the white water over the rocks and shallows. He remembered the water churning around his legs when he waded out with the other boys in the summer. But just then, Andreas entered the shop and all of Petrescu's daydreams came tumbling down.

"Those bells! I must have those bells!" called Andreas toward the dim interior of the shop, for he didn't see Petrescu at first, it was so dark in there.

"Bells?" asked Petrescu. "We have all kinds of bells. State, please, whether you desire a dinner bell, a sleigh bell, a doorbell, a bell from a locomotive of which I have three, a steamboat bell of which I have one, a cowbell, goat bell, cat bell, horse bell, school bell, or church bell. Please speak up. I lost my hearing in the Turkish War."

"Horse bells," said Andreas, without hesitation. "The horse bells I just heard."

"Church bells it is," said Petrescu. "I have three most beautiful bells in my backyard. If you will so kindly step this—"

"HORSE BELLS!" shouted Andreas.

"Ah yes," said the owner. "Very good. Is it for a Belgian draft horse, a Cleveland Bay, a Shire, an Arabian Charger, a Percheron, or a Lipizzaner? I recommend to you, sir, the Lipizzaner, a most noble breed of horse which my father once owned. It comes from my own part of the world. A most marvelous horse—"

"But I don't want a horse! I want bells! BELLS! HORSE BELLS!" shouted Andreas.

"Good. Good. Here is horse bells. The best antique horse bells, from Hungary. With bells like these, you will sing as you go."

"I have to try them, first," said Andreas. He took the leather harness with the bells on it, carried it to the door of the shop, and shook the bells. They had a pleasing enough sound, but Socrates stood with his head lower than ever.

"No good!" said Andreas. "No good! What other bells do you have?"

And one at a time, Andreas tried all the bells in the shop: dinner bells, sleigh bells, locomotive bells, cow-, goat, cat, horse, and school bells. But Socrates

didn't lift his head a single inch.

"I must see your other bells!" shouted Andreas. "The bells I heard before!"

"You've tried all the bells in my shop," said Petrescu. "What do you want? Do you expect your horse to dance when you ring my bells? Do you want him to sing?"

"I want him to raise his head."

"Speak up! Speak up! I was a cannoneer in the Turkish War and I no longer hear people whisper."

"I WANT HIM TO RAISE HIS HEAD!"

"Ah, that's different," said Petrescu. "Trouble with your horse? Be so kind as to let *me* have a look. My father was a horse expert; I learned *everything* from him."

And Petrescu went out to the street and examined Socrates even more thoroughly than Dr. Withers had done. When he was finished, he shook his head and sighed.

"What is it? What is it?" asked Andreas.

"Most simple. We see it often in Rumania. Your horse is bewitched. I don't know how; I don't know who. Gypsies? Do you have friends who are gypsies? Never mind. You need special bells. Magic bells. *Sssh*. I have some."

"You've been hiding them!" shouted Andreas,

very loudly, so Petrescu would hear. "Are *those* the bells I heard before?"

"Very likely. Very likely. Because magic bells can ring even when they're silent . . . ahh . . . where did I put them? *Hmmm* . . . "

Petrescu searched through piles of furniture and lamps and books and boxes, and as he searched he murmured to himself, "Ah, from Italy, a very good chair . . . Ah, so there you are, the complete works of Shakespeare in Bulgarian . . . *Mmm*, Bucharest, music box with glass top, beautiful . . . Ah ha, so that's where that lamp was. . . . Here! Here they are! I have them! The magic bells!"

And Petrescu brought out a metal box and placed it on the counter. He blew the dust off the cover, then opened the box carefully. And inside, Andreas saw a set of six shiny silver bells on a long red cord. Each bell was a different size and each had little pictures of birds and flowers engraved on it.

"Ahhh," said Andreas, "they are like gems. Quick! Let me try them!"

"No, no, no," said Petrescu. "*I* will try them." And Petrescu carried the bells out to the horse and held them under Socrates' muzzle so that he could see the bells and smell them.

"See, horse!" called Petrescu. "These are the bells

of Deva in Rumania. At the sound of these bells, every evil spell will go back up into the sky, like mist. Vampires will become little bats—harmless, lovable bats. Yes. You have nothing to fear, horse. When I ring the bells, the demons in you will fight each other to leave. One sneeze, horse, and they will be gone."

And Petrescu rang the bells, gently, delicately, next to Socrates' right ear, next to Socrates' left ear, and, finally, directly in front of Socrates' forehead. But Socrates didn't move a muscle; he didn't even flick his tail. Then Petrescu rang the bells louder, left ear, right ear, forehead. Nothing. Petrescu shook the bells with all his might, and the red cord snapped. The bells flew through the air in every direction and bounced and jingle-jangled on the pavement. Socrates stood with his head down, scarcely blinking his eyes.

"Your horse has ruined my bells!" shouted Petrescu. "That stupid beast! He is too stupid to be cured! Too stupid to sneeze out the demons! Take him away before I lose my temper!"

Petrescu dashed back and forth, picking up the loose bells and calling, "Oh bells of Deva, pay no attention to that stupid horse! Come back to sleep in your box! We will find you a better horse to cure."

But just then a strange thing happened. A slight sound of bells came from the direction of Petrescu's shop. It sounded just like the tinkling bells that Andreas had heard earlier. And immediately Socrates' ears twitched and up came his head.

"There! That's *it!"* Andreas called out.

"What? Where?" Petrescu asked, bewildered.

At that moment, a little boy of two toddled out of the shop, pulling a wooden cart on a long string. In the front of the cart were three little bells, toy bells that were tapped by little metal hammers whenever the wheels of the cart turned. The little bells tinkled as merrily as a running brook.

"What!" said Petrescu. "But that's just Nicolae. My little grandson, Nicolae. He must have been playing in the backyard and—" Petrescu suddenly realized that the horse's head was up high. He looked from his grandson to the horse and back, completely baffled. Had anything like this ever happened back in Rumania?

"It's impossible!" said Petrescu. "Impossible! There is a mistake somewhere. Your horse is mistaken. . . . Wait, wait! Let me think. . . ."

"I want to buy your grandson's cart," said Andreas. "Name your price!"

But Petrescu was lost in thought. "Ah ha!" he said, suddenly. "I have it! Yes, yes! That's it! Your horse is cured. Cured! I've seen it happen in Rumania. My

bells have transferred *their* magic to *Nicolae's* bells!
Yes, it is not unusual. In Rumania, all the bells talk
to one another. They learn each other's secrets. And
when they talk to *gypsy* bells . . . Ah, but never
mind. The demons have been expelled. Your horse
is cured."

Petrescu gave his grandson, Nicolae, a dinner bell
and a goat bell in exchange for the toy cart. Then
Petrescu sold the toy cart with its bells to Andreas
for thirty cents and a pair of used trousers from the
pile of old clothes. Everyone seemed satisfied, includ-
ing Socrates.

Andreas tied the toy cart to his wagon and pulled
it behind like a caboose on a train. The little cart
jingled and tinkled all day long, as it bounced over
the cobbles. And Socrates went clip-clop-clip-clop-
clip-clop quickly along the street, with his head held
high.

"Good horse! Good horse!" Andreas called. "Yes,
the bells have magic in them. Even *I* feel younger.
Come, let's go up Second Avenue. We'll show the
vegetable man a thing or two. *And* the fruit man.
We'll show *everyone*!"

And so, had you lived back then, you might have
seen the old-clothes man go proudly by in his wagon,
pulling a child's cart behind, and calling: *"Yaa!*

Young old clothes! Young old clothes! *Yaaa!*" Your mother or father might have noticed him, too, though they undoubtedly would have mentioned that he seemed to be in his second childhood, poor fellow, with that toy cart and rather foolish call.

But *you* would have known better, because the story of the magic bells would have reached your ears, as it reached the ears of all the children of the Lower East Side. For Andreas had told the story to Mario Basuto, the vegetable man, who told it to his son, Joey, who told it to his friend Vincent DeMarco, who told it to Cathy Dunn, who in turn told it to Aaron Kandel. And Aaron, who always loved mystery and magic, would most likely have told it to you.

Mrs. Dunn's Lovely, Lovely Farm

MRS. Dunn had always wanted a farm. Back in the old country, she had lived in the great city of Dublin with its crowded streets and noisy carts over the cobblestones, with its men forever looking for work, and its thin children, forever hungry.

She had made her husband promise that when they came to America they would save every penny they possibly could, so that in time they could buy a farm. A lovely farm with chickens and cows and potatoes, with the smell of sweet clover and the giggle of a brook always beyond the door. Where their children, Cathy and Neil, could have good fresh food, could grow and run and tumble. A lovely, lovely farm.

When they arrived in New York, with other

thousands from Ireland and Italy and Hungary and Russia, they moved into a little apartment on the third floor of a building near Second Avenue. One of their neighbors was named DeMarco and another was named Kandel. In Dublin everyone had Irish names; this was something new and different, and a little frightening. But the neighbors said hello and smiled and warned them about Mr. Warfield, the terrible, horrible landlord. And Mr. and Mrs. Dunn felt much better, because in Dublin the landlords had been terrible and horrible, too. Things were becoming familiar very quickly.

The next task was for Mr. Dunn to find work. After much searching, he found a job hauling coal. He helped send the coal roaring like a river down a metal chute into the basements of buildings. Sometimes he would stand on the mound of coal in the back of the truck and coax it down through a square hole into the chute. And sometimes he would stand on the coal pile down in the cellar, clearing the coal away from the bottom of the chute so that more coal and still more coal could come roaring down into the coal bin.

Mr. Dunn would come home every night looking just like a great lump of coal, himself. But after a good washing and a hot dinner, Mr. Dunn looked almost like Mr. Dunn again.

And though they could pay the rent and buy coats for the winter, and could afford a little more lamb and butter than they could in Dublin, they couldn't seem to save much money. After a year, Mrs. Dunn counted four dollars and ninety-two cents in her secret empty cereal box, and Mr. Dunn had eight dollars and twelve cents in his shaving mug.

At that rate, they would never have enough for a farm. There were new shoes needed, and a new blanket, and a bigger stew pot, and this, and that, and the other. So Mrs. Dunn made a firm decision. They must buy their farm now, as much of it as they could, or the money would vanish like a mist over the chimneys of Dublin. And Mr. Dunn had to admit she was right.

That very next day, Mrs. Dunn bought a hen. They had told her at the market that it was a good dependable laying hen, a Rhode Island Red, the best. Mrs. Dunn wrapped the hen in a scarf, tucked it under her arm, and carried it five blocks back to her kitchen. Then she put the hen on the floor and watched it strut on the yellow linoleum.

The children named it Amelia for no special reason, and fed it cereal and corn and crusts of bread. Mr. Dunn brought home scraps of wood from the coal yard and built a coop. Then with more wood and some chicken wire, he built a little barnyard filled with dirt and pebbles in which Amelia could scratch. And he took some old felt hats and shaped them into nice, soft nests.

Soon, Amelia was joined by Agatha, and then Adeline. Now there were two eggs, sometimes three, every morning in the hat-nests, fresh and delicious. Cathy and Neil loved Agatha and Amelia and Adeline as if they were their own sisters. Each hen was different: Amelia was very, very proud and strutted as if she were a rooster; Agatha was a busybody, forever poking into everything; Adeline was shy and loved to sit in the coop and preen. Soon, the other children in the building started bringing the three hens little presents: Aaron Kandel brought pieces of a huge, flat, dry cracker called *matzo* which Adeline particularly loved; Fred Reinhardt brought scraps of thick pumpernickel bread; and Vincent DeMarco brought dried seeds called chick peas. And sometimes, Mrs. Dunn would give one of the children a freshly laid egg to take home.

Now, it was time for the vegetables, for who ever heard of a farm without vegetables? Mr. Dunn built large, deep boxes, filled them with earth, and planted seeds. Then he put them on the fire escape outside the bedroom window. When the fire-escape landing was covered with boxes, he put new boxes on the iron stairs leading up to the next landing. Soon, the fire escape was blooming with the green shoots of tomato plants, string beans, potatoes, onions, and parsley. And on every windowsill were pots of spices: rosemary, thyme, mint, chives.

On weekdays, Mrs. Dunn carefully weeded and watered the fire-escape garden and fed the chickens. And on Sundays, after he had tried to wash the last of the coal from his face and hands for the third time, Mr. Dunn would repair the chicken wire, and prop up the growing vegetables with tall sticks and string, and build new boxes. Then he and Mrs. Dunn would walk from room to room, admiring the pots of spices, the vegetables, the chickens, and the mushrooms growing in flat boxes on the kitchen shelves.

But one day, Mr. Warfield, the terrible, horrible landlord came to collect the rents. As he was about to enter the building, a sun shower drenched his hat. He took off the hat and looked at it with disbelief, for there wasn't a cloud in the sky. Perhaps a tenant had spilled some dishwater on him, from above. He looked up and shook his fist toward the top of the building, at the hidden enemy.

His mouth dropped in astonishment and he forgot

to bring down his fist, for up above, three stories up, was a hanging garden twining about the metal bars of the fire escape. A lady was watering the green mirage with a watering can, and some of it had dripped down the fire escape from landing to landing until it finally splashed on Mr. Warfield's head.

"This is an outrage!" Mr. Warfield muttered to himself. "It's completely unreasonable."

Then he plunged into the building and rushed toward the stairs.

"Ah, Mr. Warfield," said Mrs. Callahan at the first landing, "and when, pray tell, are you going to fix m'stove? The divil of a thing's got only one burner working. Do you expect me to pay m'rent when I can't cook soup and stew at the same time?"

"Oh blast!" said Mr. Warfield. "I'll see you later. I've got a madhouse here. A madhouse! Let me go by, Mrs. Callahan."

"And what might be the trouble, if I may ask?" said Mrs. Callahan.

"Somebody's growing a tree on the fire escape!"

"Ah, to be sure, to be sure." And with that, Mrs. Callahan nudged her little girl, Noreen, standing next to her. Without a word, Noreen turned and raced up the two flights of stairs to warn her friend Cathy Dunn that Warfield, the monster landlord,

51

was on his way up. "And tell me now, Mr. Warfield, but how would a tree gain the necessary nourishment on a fire escape, do you know?"

"I intend to find out, Mrs. Callahan, if you'll let me get by!"

"But m'stove, Mr. Warfield. I'm paying rent for three rooms and four burners."

"Yes, yes, yes, yes! Very reasonable request. We'll have it fixed in seventy-two hours. Now please let me get—"

"Seventy-two hours, is it? Make it twenty-four," said Mrs. Callahan.

"But that's only one *day*. That's unreasonable. Make it . . . forty-eight hours."

"Thirty-six, Mr. Warfield, or I'll have the Board of Health, I will."

"Forty!"

"Thirty-eight!"

"All right! We'll have it fixed within thirty-eight hours! Now let me *through*!"

And Mr. Warfield raced up the flight of stairs to the second landing.

"Hello, Mr. Warfield!" Mrs. Grotowski called. "I dreamt about you last night! And what did I dream?"

"I don't care!" said Mr. Warfield. "Let me go by!"

"I'll *tell* you what. I dreamt that I took the money

for your rent and tore it up into little shreds. Then I put a little pepper on it, a little salt, stirred in some nice chicken fat, and made you eat every dollar of it until you choked. And *why*?"

"Please, Mrs. Grotowski! This isn't the time for your dreams!"

"I'll tell you why. Because you promised to have my apartment painted two months ago. Two months! Where are the painters? Did they join the Foreign Legion? Or is it possible that they've gone over Niagara Falls in a barrel?"

"We'll have the painters soon."

"When?"

"Soon. Very soon."

"How soon?"

"Very, very soon. Let me go by, Mrs. Grotowski, before I lose my temper."

"This week! I want them *this* week."

"Next week."

"By Friday!"

"By next Wednesday, Mrs. Grotowski."

"By next Monday, Mr. Warfield."

"Tuesday."

"All right. But it better be Tuesday," said Mrs. Grotowski.

"Tuesday. Absolutely, positively Tuesday."

Meanwhile, up in the Dunns' apartment, people were flying back and forth. Cathy and Neil had each grabbed a chicken and raced out the door. One chicken went into the DeMarco apartment, the other clucked away in Mrs. Kandel's kitchen. But the chicken left behind, Amelia—or was it Adeline?—had gotten so excited from all the rushing about that she'd flown up to the ceiling and was now roosting comfortably on top of the chandelier in the living room. Mr. Dunn wasn't at home, but Mrs. Dunn took vegetable boxes off the fire-escape landing and slid them under the bed. And from the apartment above, Mrs. Cherney climbed out of her bedroom window onto the fire escape, took more boxes off the iron stairs, and hid them in her own apartment. But try though they did, there just wasn't enough time to hide everything.

For Mr. Warfield had finally reached the third floor and was pounding at the Dunns' door. Three Rhode Island Reds answered with a cascade of *berawk-bawk-bawk*s: one in Mrs. Kandel's kitchen, one in Mrs. DeMarco's bathroom and one on Mrs. Dunn's chandelier. But fortunately, Mr. Warfield knew they weren't chickens, because that would be impossible. It was the children making chicken noises at him. Why did they all hate him? He was a good man. Fair.

Reasonable. Wasn't he always reasonable? . . . But what was *this*? There were feathers in the hallway. Children having a pillow fight? Very likely. Ah well, children must play. No harm. Not like trees on the fire escape!

Then Mr. Warfield pounded on the door again; not the dainty tap-tap of a salesman, nor the thump-thump of a bill collector, but the Shaboom-Shaboom of a landlord. And again, from three apartments, three children in a superb imitation of three chickens, *berawk-bawk*ed away at Mr. Warfield.

Why? thought Mr. Warfield. Why? He had three children of his own and they *loved* him. Didn't they? Of course they did.

At last the door opened a crack, and Mrs. Dunn's hand appeared with an envelope holding the rent money. She waved the envelope up and down at Mr. Warfield. Mr. Warfield took the envelope, but also pushed firmly on the door.

"Mrs. Dunn, I'd like a word or two with you," he said.

"I'm feeling a bit ill today, Mr. Warfield, sir. Would you be so kindly as to stop back next week."

"Mrs. Dunn! There is a tree growing on your fire escape!"

"Oh, Mr. Warfield," said Mrs. Dunn, "and is it

the bottle you've been having with all that rent money?"

"I am not *drunk*, Mrs. Dunn! I have two *eyes*!"

"So you have, Mr. Warfield," said Mrs. Dunn rapidly. "You're blessed. There's many a blind man would trade this very building for your keen eyesight. But still, a tree cannot truly grow on a fire escape. Unless, of course, it's the will of God. With which you would not want to tamper, Mr. Warfield, would you? Good day to you now."

"Good day my foot! I demand to see the condition of that fire escape. As landlord, I have the right to enter and inspect the premises at reasonable hours. I'm a reasonable man and I would never come at an unreasonable hour."

"Why it's nearly four o' the clock. I've got to do m' husband's supper. 'Tis not a reasonable hour at all," said Mrs. Dunn.

"Either you let me enter, madam, or I'll call the police. *And* the fire department. A tree on the fire escape is a fire hazard. Let me in!"

"Tomorrow."

"NOW!" shouted Mr. Warfield. And with that, the chicken on the chandelier clucked again. "Did you hear that, Mrs. Dunn?"

"Sounded like a cuckoo clock. Cuckoo, cuckoo. 'Tis four o' the clock, you see."

"Nonsense. You have a *chicken* in there! My building has *chickens*!" At that, all three hens in all three apartments *berawk-bawk*ed again. "This isn't an apartment house! It's a lunatic asylum!" Then Mr. Warfield pushed his way past Mrs. Dunn and stormed into her living room.

"My chandelier!" shouted Mr. Warfield.

" 'Tisn't *your* chandelier. I've paid the rent. 'Tis *my* chandelier," said Mrs. Dunn.

Mr. Warfield rushed through to the bedroom and stared at the remains of the farm on the fire escape. "My fire escape!" His face was flushed, his eyes were bulging. "Unbelievable! Mrs. Dunn, what are these weeds supposed to *be*?"

"That? Why that's onions, Mr. Warfield."

"*This* is an *onion*?"

"Oh, you can't see it. The onion's beneath the dirt. Least I hope 'tis."

"And *this*?" he said, pointing.

"That's supposed to be potatoes. But I fear for them. The soil's not deep enough."

"Incredible!" he said. "Don't you like geraniums, Mrs. Dunn? I thought ladies liked to grow geraniums. Look out the window, across the street. See the windowsills? There and there. And over there. Everyone *else* is growing geraniums."

"That's a good *idea,* Mr. Warfield," said Mrs. Dunn. " 'Twould brighten up the house. I'll fetch some seed tomorrow."

"No, no. I didn't mean . . . Mrs. Dunn, look here. This is a firetrap! And that chicken—"

"I have two more, visiting with the neighbors."

"Well, that, Mrs. Dunn, is a relief. I thought *all* the tenants had gone insane."

"No, 'tis only m'self. But I do think I'm as sane as you, if not a bit saner. Because you see, I shall have the freshest vegetables in the city of New York. I already have the freshest eggs."

"Those chickens, in an apartment, are a health hazard. You'll have to remove them! Sell them to a farmer or a butcher."

"I shan't. They stay right here."

"That's unreasonable. I'm a reasonable man, Mrs. Dunn. Say something reasonable, *ask* something reasonable, and I'll say: *that's* reasonable."

"Very well. Why don't you pretend that you hadn't come at all today. Then you wouldn't have seen anything, would you, and your mind would rest easy," said Mrs. Dunn.

58

"Completely unreasonable! And *that's* why you tenants don't like me. Because *I'm* reasonable, and you're all *un*reasonable. Simple as that."

"Oh, I like you, Mr. Warfield."

"Nonsense."

"Any landlord who would offer me the use of his roof for a fine little garden must be a very likable *and* reasonable man."

"I didn't offer you any roof, Mrs. Dunn."

"You were going to. I saw it on the tip of your lips."

"My *lips?*"

"And you were going to say how much better 'twould be if the chickens had a much bigger coop up there on the roof."

"*I* was never going to say—"

"Tut tut, Mr. Warfield," said Mrs. Dunn. "You've as good as said it. And I was going to answer that for such generosity you should surely receive some fresh string beans and onions and potatoes in season. And you were going to say, 'Ah, and how lovely the roof would look with greenery all about.' And I was about to answer, 'Yes, Mr. Warfield, and the tenants would surely look at you most affectionately.' Would they not, now?"

"*Hmm,*" said Mr. Warfield, thinking.

"Reasonable or unreasonable?" asked Mrs. Dunn.

"*Hmm* . . . well . . . I'd have to give this some thought."

"But you're a man of *action,* Mr. Warfield. You pound on the door like a very tiger."

"Yes. Well . . . it's not *un*reasonable," said Mr. Warfield. "If you didn't already *have* any chickens or trees or onions, I would say no. But since you *do* have all this *jungle* of creatures and vines . . . I would, after careful consideration, being after all a human being, I would . . . *ahem, ahem* . . . say . . . *ahem* . . . yes."

"Oh, you are a darling man, Mr. Warfield. A darling, *darling* man."

"Here, Mrs. Dunn! Watch your language! I mean to say! *Darling* man?"

"Oh, back in the old country, it only means you're nice, that's all."

"Oh. Now remember, Mrs. Dunn, a bargain's a bargain. I expect one tenth of everything you grow as my roof rent. Is that a deal?"

" 'Tis a deal."

"Except the onions. You can keep them all. I hate onions. My whole family hates onions."

And with that, Mr. Warfield slammed his hat on his head, only to find it was still wet from Mrs. Dunn's

watering can. Without a word, he turned and stalked out to the living room. At that moment, Amelia—or was it Adeline?—up on the chandelier decided it was time to come down. For there, on top of Mr. Warfield's head, was her nest-shaped-like-a-hat, moving by. And down she came, wings beating, feathers flying, on top of Mr. Warfield's head. "Oh blast!" shouted Mr. Warfield as he raced to the hallway with the chicken flapping on top of him.

"She likes you!" called Mrs. Dunn. "She knows you have a good heart! Chickens can tell right off!"

But Mr. Warfield didn't hear this very clearly, for as he raced out to the hallway and down the stairs, all three chickens started their *berawk-bawk*ing again, and the loudest of all was the one on top of Mr. Warfield. He finally escaped by leaving his nest-shaped-like-a-hat, behind.

And so Mrs. Dunn moved everything to the roof, and Mr. Dunn added still more boxes for vegetables. Cathy and Neil and their friends went up to the roof every afternoon to feed the chickens and water the plants. And Mrs. Dunn had her lovely, lovely farm—or at least she thought she did, which comes to the same thing in the end.

Keplik, the Match Man

THERE once was a little old man who lived in a big old tenement on Second Avenue. His name was Mr. Keplik and he had once been a watchmaker. In the window of his tiny watch-repair shop he had put up a sign that read: WHEN YOUR WRIST WATCH WON'T TICK, IT'S TIME FOR KEPLIK. Keplik loved watches and clocks and had loved repairing them. If a clock he was repairing stopped ticking he would say to himself, "Eh, eh, eh, it's dying." And when it started ticking again he would say, "I am *gebentsht*. I am blessed. It's alive."

Whenever an elevated train rumbled by overhead, Keplik would have to put down his delicate work, for his workbench and the entire shop would shake and vibrate. But Keplik would close his eyes and say, "Never mind. There are worse things. How many people back in Lithuania wouldn't give their right eye to have a watch-repair shop under an el train in America."

While he worked Keplik never felt lonely, for there were always customers coming in with clocks and watches and complaints.

"My watch was supposed to be ready last week," a customer would say. "I need my watch! Will you have it ready by tonight, Keplik?"

And Keplik would answer, "Maybe yes, maybe no. It depends on how many el trains pass by during the rush hour." And he would point his finger up toward the el structure above.

But when Keplik grew very old, he had to give up watch repairing, for he could no longer climb up and down the three flights of stairs to his apartment. He became very lonely, for there were no longer any customers to visit him and complain. And his hands felt empty and useless for there were no longer any gears or pivots or hairsprings or mainsprings to repair. "Terrible," said Keplik, to himself. "I'm too young to be old. I will take up a hobby. Perhaps I should build a clock out of walnut shells. Or make a rose garden out of red crepe paper and green silk. Or make a windmill out of wooden matchsticks. I'll see what I have in the house."

There were no walnuts and no crepe paper, but there were lots and lots of burned matchsticks, for, in those days, the gas stoves had to be lit with a match every time you wanted a scrambled egg or a cup of hot cocoa. So Keplik started to build a little windmill out of matches.

Within a month's time, the windmill was finished. Keplik put it on his kitchen table and started to blow like the east wind. The arms turned slowly, then faster, just like a real windmill. "I'm gebentsht," said Keplik. "It's alive."

Next, Keplik decided to make a castle, complete with a drawbridge. But the matches were expensive; he would need hundreds and hundreds for a castle. So he put a little sign outside his apartment door, and another in his window: USED MATCHSTICKS BOUGHT HERE. A PENNY FOR FIFTY. IF YOU HAVE A MATCHSTICK, SELL IT TO KEPLIK.

The word spread up and down the block very quickly, and soon there were children at Keplik's door with bags and boxes of used matches. Keplik showed them the windmill on the kitchen table and invited them to blow like the east wind. And Keplik was happy, because he had visitors again and lots of work for his hands.

Day after day, week after week, Keplik glued and fitted the matches together. And finally the castle stood completed, with red and blue flags flying from every turret. The children brought toy soldiers and laid siege to the castle, while Keplik pulled up the drawbridge.

Next, Keplik made a big birdcage out of matches, and put a real canary in it. The bird sang and flew back and forth while the delicate cage swung on its hook. "Ah ha," said Keplik. "The cage is alive. And so is the canary. I am double gebentsht."

Then he made little airplanes and jewelry boxes from matchsticks and gave them to the boys and girls who visited him. And the children began calling him "the Match Man."

One day, Keplik decided that it was time for a masterpiece. "I am at my heights as an artist," Keplik said to himself. "No more windmills. No more bird-cages. I am going to make the Woolworth Building. Or the Eiffel Tower. Or the Brooklyn Bridge. Eh . . . eh . . . but which?"

And after much thought, he decided that a bridge would be better than a tower or a skyscraper, because if he built a bridge he wouldn't have to cut a hole in the ceiling. The Brooklyn Bridge would be his masterpiece. It would run across the living room from the kitchen to the bedroom, and the two towers would stand as high as his head. "For this I need matches!" Keplik said aloud. "Matches! I must have matches."

And he posted a new sign: MATCH FOR MATCH, YOU CANNOT MATCH KEPLIK'S PRICE FOR USED MATCHES. ONE CENT FOR FIFTY. HURRY! HURRY! HURRY!

Vincent DeMarco, who lived around the corner, brought fifty matches that very afternoon, and Cathy Dunn and Noreen Callahan brought a hundred matches each the next morning. Day after day, the matches kept coming, and day after day, Keplik the Match Man glued and fixed and bent and pressed the matches into place.

The bridge was so complicated that Keplik had decided to build it in separate sections, and then join all the sections afterward. The bridge's support towers, the end spans, and the center span slowly took shape in different parts of the room. The room seemed to grow smaller as the bridge grew larger. A masterpiece, thought Keplik. There is no longer room for me to sit in my favorite chair. But I must have more matches! It's time to build the cables!

Even the long support cables were made from matchsticks, split and glued and twisted together. Keplik would twist the sticks until his fingers grew numb. Then he would go into the kitchen to make a cup of coffee for himself, not so much for the coffee, but for the fact that lighting the stove would provide him with yet another matchstick. And sometimes, as he was drinking his coffee, he would get up and take a quick look at his bridge, because it always looked different when he was away from it for awhile. "It's beginning to be alive," he would say.

And then one night, it was time for the great final step. The towers and spans and cables all had to be joined together to give the finished structure. A most difficult job. For everything was supported from the cables above, as in a real bridge, and all the final connections had to be glued and tied almost at the same moment. Nothing must shift or slip for a full half hour, until the glue dried thoroughly.

Keplik worked carefully, his watchmaker's hands steadily gluing and pressing strut after strut, cable after cable. The end spans were in place. The center span was ready. Glue, press, glue, press. Then suddenly, an el train rumbled by outside. The ground trembled, the old tenement shivered as it always did, the windows rattled slightly, and the center span slid from its glued moorings. Then one of the end cables vibrated loose, then another, and the bridge slipped slowly apart into separate spans and towers. "Eh, eh, eh," said Keplik. "It's dying."

Keplik tried again, but another train hurtled past from the other direction. And again the bridge slowly slipped apart. I am too tired, thought Keplik. I'll try again tomorrow.

Keplik decided to wait until late the next night, when there would be fewer trains. But again, as the bridge was almost completed, a train roared past, the house shook, and everything slipped apart. Again and again, Keplik tried, using extra supports and tying parts together. But the bridge seemed to enjoy waiting for the next train to shake it apart again.

Ah me, thought Keplik. All my life those el trains shook the watches in my hands, down below in my shop. All my life I said things could be worse; how many people back in Lithuania wouldn't give their left foot to have a watch-repair shop under an el train in America.

But why do the el trains have to follow me three flights up? Why can't they leave me alone in my old age? When I die, will there be an el train over my grave? Will I be shaken and rattled around while I'm trying to take a little well-deserved snooze? And when I reach heaven, will there be an el train there, too, so I can't even play a nice, soothing tune on a harp without all this *tummel*, this noise? It's much too much for me. This is it. The end. The bridge will be a masterpiece in parts. The Brooklyn Bridge after an earthquake.

At that moment, another el train roared by and Keplik the Match Man called toward the train, "One thing I'll *never* do! I'll never make an el train out of matches! Never! How do you like *that*!"

When the children came the next afternoon, to see if the bridge was finished at last, Keplik told them of his troubles with the el trains. "The bridge, my children, is *farpotshket*. You know what that means? A mess!"

The children made all sorts of suggestions: hold it this way, fix it that way, glue it here, tie it there. But to all of them, Keplik the Match Man shook his head. "Impossible. I've tried that. Nothing works."

Then Vincent DeMarco said, "My father works on an el station uptown. He knows all the motormen, he says. Maybe he can get them to stop the trains."

Keplik laughed. "Ah, such a nice idea. But not even God can stop the Second Avenue el."

"I'll bet my father can," said Vincent.

"Bet he can't," said Joey Basuto. And just then,

a train sped by: raketa, raketa, raketa, raketa, raketa. "The trains never stop for nothing," said Joey.

And the children went home for dinner, disappointed that the bridge made from all their matchsticks was farpoot . . . farbot . . . *whatever* that word was. A mess.

Vincent told his father, but Mr. DeMarco shrugged. "No. Impossible. Impossible," he said. "I'm not important enough."

"But couldn't you *try*?" pleaded Vincent.

"I know *one* motorman. So what good's that, huh? One motorman. All I do is make change in the booth."

"Maybe he'll tell everybody else."

"*Assurdità.* Nonsense. They have more to worry about than Mr. Keplik's bridge. Eat your soup!"

But Mr. DeMarco thought to himself that if he did happen to see his friend, the motorman, maybe, just for a laugh, he'd mention it. . . .

Two days later, Vincent ran upstairs to Keplik's door and knocked. *Tonight* his father had said! Tonight at one A.M.! Keplik couldn't believe his ears. The trains would stop for his bridge? It couldn't be. Someone was playing a joke on Vincent's father.

But that night, Keplik prepared, just in case it was true. Everything was ready: glue, thread, supports, towers, spans, cables.

71

A train clattered by at five minutes to one. Then silence. Rapidly, rapidly, Keplik worked. Press, glue, press, glue. One cable connected. Two cables. Three. Four. First tower finished. Fifth cable connected. Sixth. Seventh. Eighth. Other tower in place. Now gently, gently. Center span in position. Glue, press, glue, press. Tie threads. Tie more threads. Easy. Easy. Everything balanced. Everything supported. Now please. No trains till it dries.

The minutes ticked by. Keplik was sweating. Still no train. The bridge was holding. The bridge was finished. And then, outside the window, he saw an el train creeping along, slowly, carefully: cla . . . keta . . . cla . . . keta . . . cla . . . keta . . . cla . . . keta . . . Then another, moving slowly from the other direction: cla . . . keta . . . cla . . . keta. . . .

And Keplik shouted toward the trains, "Thank you, Mister Motorman! Tomorrow, I am going to start a great new masterpiece! The Second Avenue el from Fourteenth Street to Delancey Street! Thank you for slowing up your trains!"

And first one motorman, then the other, blew his train whistle as the trains moved on, into the night beyond. "Ah, how I am gebentsht," said Keplik to himself. "In America there are kind people everywhere. All my life, the el train has shaken my hands.

But tonight, it has shaken my heart."

Keplik worked for the rest of the night on a little project. And the next morning, Keplik hung this sign made from matches outside his window, where every passing el train motorman could see it:

The Fish Angel

NOREEN Callahan was convinced that her father's fish store on Second Avenue was, without a doubt, the ugliest fish store on the East Side. The sawdust on the floor was always slimy with fish drippings; the fish were piled in random heaps on the ice; the paint on the walls was peeling off in layers; even the cat sleeping in the window was filthy. Mr. Callahan's apron was always dirty, and he wore an old battered hat that was in worse shape than the cat, if such a thing were possible. Often, fish heads would drop on the floor right under the customers' feet, and Mr. Callahan wouldn't bother to sweep them up. And as time passed, most of his customers went elsewhere for their fish.

Mr. Callahan had never wanted to sell fish in a fish store. He had wanted to be an actor, to do great, heroic, marvelous things on the stage. He tried, but was unsuccessful, and had to come back to work in his father's fish store, the store which was now his. But he took no pride in it; for what beauty was possible, what marvelous, heroic things could be done in a fish store?

Noreen's mother helped in the store most of the week, but Saturday was Noreen's day to help while her mother cleaned the house. To Noreen, it was the worst day of the week. She was ashamed to be seen in the store by any of her friends and classmates, ashamed of the smells, ashamed of the fish heads and fish tails, ashamed of the scruffy cat, and of her father's dirty apron. To Noreen, the fish store seemed a scar across her face, a scar she'd been born with.

And like a scar, Noreen carried the fish store with her everywhere, even into the schoolroom. *Fish Girl! Fish Girl! Dirty Fish Girl!* some of the girls would call her. When they did, Noreen wished she could run into the dark clothes closet at the back of the room and cry. And once or twice, she did.

But pleasant things also happened to Noreen. A few weeks before Christmas, Noreen was chosen to play an angel in the church pageant, an angel who would hover high, high up on a platform above everyone's head. And best of all, she would get to wear a beautiful, beautiful angel's gown. As beautiful as her mother could make it.

Mrs. Callahan worked on the angel's gown every night, sewing on silver spangles that would shine a thousand different ways in the light. And to go with the gown, she made a sparkling crown, a tiara, out of cloth and cardboard and gold paint and bits of clear glass.

On the day of the pageant, Noreen shone almost like a real angel, and she felt so happy and light that with just a little effort she might have flown like a real angel, too. And after the pageant, Noreen's mother and father had a little party for her in their living room. Mr. Callahan had borrowed a camera to take pictures of Noreen in her angel's gown. "To last me at least a year of looking," he said.

For though Mr. Callahan hated his fish store, he loved Noreen with a gigantic love. He often told Noreen that some children were the apple of their father's eye, but she was not only the apple of his eye, but the peach, pear, plum, and apricot, too.

And Noreen would ask, "And strawberry?"

"Yes, b'God," her father would say. "You're the fruit salad of m' eye, that's what you are. Smothered in whipped cream."

And so he took picture after picture after picture with the big old camera that slid in and out on a wooden frame. Noreen had a wonderful time posing with her friend Cathy, who had also been an angel in the pageant. But the party came to an end as all parties must, and it was time to take off the angel's gown and the tiara, and become Noreen Callahan again. How heavy Noreen felt after so much lightness and shining. Into the drawer, neatly folded, went the heavenly angel. "Perhaps next year," her mother said, "we'll have it out again."

That night, Noreen dreamed that she was dancing at a splendid ball in her dress of silver and her crown of gold. Round and round the ballroom she went, as silver spangles fluttered down like snow, turning everything into a shimmering fairy's web of light. And then she was up on her toes in a graceful pirouette. Everyone watched; everyone applauded. As she whirled, her dress opened out like a great white flower around her and . . . suddenly she felt herself sliding and skidding helplessly. She looked down; the silver spangles had changed to fish scales. The floor was covered with fish heads and fish tails and slimy, slippery sawdust. And everyone was calling: *Fish Girl! Fish Girl! Fish Girl!*

Noreen awoke, not knowing quite where she was for a moment. Then she turned over in the bed and cried and cried, till she finally fell asleep again.

The next week passed in a blur of rain and snow that instantly turned to slush. Every day, when she came home from school, Noreen looked at the dress lying in the drawer. *Wear me, wear me,* it seemed to say. But Noreen just sighed and shut the drawer, only to open it and look again an hour later.

And then, all too soon, it was Saturday. The day Noreen dreaded. Fish store day. How she wished she could turn into a real angel and just fly away.

Suddenly Noreen sat down on her bed. She knew it was decided before she could actually think. The angel gown! How could anyone wait a year to have it out again. She would wear it now. Now! In her father's store. And then people would know that she had nothing to do with that dirty apron and filthy floor. And perhaps those children would stop calling her Fish Girl. She would be a Fish Angel now.

Mrs. Callahan saw the gown under Noreen's coat, as Noreen was about to leave the house. She rarely scolded Noreen, but this was too much! It was completely daft! That gown would be ruined; her father would be very angry. Everyone would laugh at her; everyone would think she was crazy! But Mrs. Callahan saw that nothing, absolutely nothing, could stop Noreen. And she finally gave in, but not before warning Noreen that next year she would have to make her own dress. An angel's gown in a fish store! Why it was almost a sin!

When Noreen arrived at the fish store and took off her coat, Mr. Callahan was busy filleting a flounder. But when he saw Noreen he gasped and nicked himself with the knife.

"*Aggh!*" he called out, and it was a cry of surprise at the gown, and anger at Noreen, and pain from the cut, all in one. He nursed his finger, not knowing what to say to Noreen in front of all those customers.

"What a lovely gown," said a woman.

"What happened?" asked another. "Is it a special occasion?"

"His daughter," whispered a third. "His daughter. Isn't she gorgeous?"

And Mr. Callahan simply couldn't be angry anymore. As the customers complimented him on how absolutely beautiful his daughter looked, he felt something he hadn't felt for a long, long time. He felt a flush of pride. Perhaps marvelous things, even heroic

things *could* be done in a fish store.

Mr. Callahan watched Noreen as she weighed and wrapped the fish, very, very carefully so as not to get a single spot on her dress. Wherever she moved, his eyes followed, as one follows the light of a candle in a dark passage.

And toward the end of the day, Mr. Callahan took off his filthy apron and his battered hat. He went to the little room in the back of the store, and returned wearing a clean, white apron.

Christmas came and passed, and New Year's, and Noreen wore her gown and tiara every Saturday. And more and more customers came to see the girl in the angel gown. Mr. Callahan put down fresh sawdust twice a day, and laid the fish out neatly in rows, and washed and cleaned the floors and window. He even cleaned the cat, and one night in January he painted the walls white as chalk. And his business began to prosper.

The children who had called Noreen *Fish Girl,* called her nothing at all for a while. But they finally found something which they seemed to think was even worse. *Fish Angel,* they called her. *Fish Angel.* But Noreen just smiled when she heard them, for she had chosen that very name for herself, a secret name, many weeks before.

And Saturday soon became Noreen's favorite day of the week, for that was the day she could work side by side with her father in what was, without a doubt, the neatest, cleanest fish store on the East Side of New York.

Aaron's Gift

AARON Kandel had come to Tompkins Square Park to roller-skate, for the streets near Second Avenue were always too crowded with children and peddlers and old ladies and baby buggies. Though few children had bicycles in those days, almost every child owned a pair of roller skates. And Aaron was, it must be said, a Class A, triple-fantastic roller skater.

Aaron skated back and forth on the wide walkway of the park, pretending he was an aviator in an air race zooming around pylons, which were actually two lampposts. During his third lap around the racecourse, he noticed a pigeon on the grass, behaving very strangely. Aaron skated to the line of benches, then climbed over onto the lawn.

The pigeon was trying to fly, but all it could manage was to flutter and turn round and round in a large circle, as if it were performing a frenzied dance. The left wing was only half open and was beating in a clumsy, jerking fashion; it was clearly broken.

Luckily, Aaron hadn't eaten the cookies he'd stuffed into his pocket before he'd gone clacking down the three flights of stairs from his apartment, his skates already on. He broke a cookie into small crumbs and tossed some toward the pigeon. "Here pidge, here pidge," he called. The pigeon spotted the cookie crumbs and, after a moment, stopped thrashing about. It folded its wings as best it could, but the broken wing still stuck half out. Then it strutted over to the crumbs, its head bobbing forth-back, forth-back, as if it were marching a little in front of the rest of the body—perfectly normal, except for that half-open wing which seemed to make the bird stagger sideways every so often.

The pigeon began eating the crumbs as Aaron quickly unbuttoned his shirt and pulled it off. Very slowly, he edged toward the bird, making little kissing sounds like the ones he heard his grandmother make when she fed the sparrows on the back fire escape.

Then suddenly Aaron plunged. The shirt, in both

hands, came down like a torn parachute. The pigeon beat its wings, but Aaron held the shirt to the ground, and the bird couldn't escape. Aaron felt under the shirt, gently, and gently took hold of the wounded pigeon.

"Yes, yes, pidge," he said, very softly. "There's a good boy. Good pigeon, good."

The pigeon struggled in his hands, but little by little Aaron managed to soothe it. "Good boy, pidge. That's your new name. Pidge. I'm gonna take you home, Pidge. Yes, yes, *ssh*. Good boy. I'm gonna fix you up. Easy, Pidge, easy does it. Easy, boy."

Aaron squeezed through an opening between the row of benches and skated slowly out of the park, while holding the pigeon carefully with both hands as if it were one of his mother's rare, precious cups from the old country. How fast the pigeon's heart was beating! Was he afraid? Or did all pigeons' hearts beat fast?

It was fortunate that Aaron was an excellent skater, for he had to skate six blocks to his apartment, over broken pavement and sudden gratings and curbs and cobblestones. But when he reached home, he asked Noreen Callahan, who was playing on the stoop, to take off his skates for him. He would not chance going up three flights on roller skates this time.

"Is he sick?" asked Noreen.

"Broken wing," said Aaron. "I'm gonna fix him up and make him into a carrier pigeon or something."

"Can I watch?" asked Noreen.

"Watch what?"

"The operation. I'm gonna be a nurse when I grow up."

"OK," said Aaron. "You can even help. You can help hold him while I fix him up."

Aaron wasn't quite certain what his mother would say about his new-found pet, but he was pretty sure he knew what his grandmother would think. His grandmother had lived with them ever since his grandfather had died three years ago. And she fed the sparrows and jays and crows and robins on the back fire escape with every spare crumb she could find. In fact, Aaron noticed that she sometimes created crumbs where they didn't exist, by squeezing and tearing pieces of her breakfast roll when his mother wasn't looking.

Aaron didn't really understand his grandmother, for he often saw her by the window having long conversations with the birds, telling them about her days as a little girl in the Ukraine. And once he saw her take her mirror from her handbag and hold it out toward the birds. She told Aaron that she wanted them to see how beautiful they were. Very strange. But

Aaron did know that she would love Pidge, because she loved everything.

To his surprise, his mother said he could keep the pigeon, temporarily, because it was sick, and we were all strangers in the land of Egypt, and it might not be bad for Aaron to have a pet. Temporarily.

The wing was surprisingly easy to fix, for the break showed clearly and Pidge was remarkably patient and still, as if he knew he was being helped. Or perhaps he was just exhausted from all the thrashing about he had done. Two Popsicle sticks served as splints, and strips from an old undershirt were used to tie them in place. Another strip held the wing to the bird's body.

Aaron's father arrived home and stared at the pigeon. Aaron waited for the expected storm. But instead, Mr. Kandel asked, "Who *did* this?"

"Me," said Aaron. "And Noreen Callahan."

"Sophie!" he called to his wife. "Did you see this! Ten years old and it's better than Dr. Belasco could do. He's a genius!"

As the days passed, Aaron began training Pidge to be a carrier pigeon. He tied a little cardboard tube to Pidge's left leg and stuck tiny rolled-up sheets of paper with secret messages into it: THE ENEMY IS ATTACKING AT DAWN. Or: THE GUNS ARE HIDDEN IN THE TRUNK OF THE CAR. Or: VINCENT DeMARCO IS

A BRITISH SPY. Then Aaron would set Pidge down at one end of the living room and put some popcorn at the other end. And Pidge would waddle slowly across the room, cooing softly, while the ends of his bandages trailed along the floor.

At the other end of the room, one of Aaron's friends would take out the message, stick a new one in, turn Pidge around, and aim him at the popcorn that Aaron put down on his side of the room.

And Pidge grew fat and contented on all the popcorn and crumbs and corn and crackers and Aaron's grandmother's breakfast rolls.

Aaron had told all the children about Pidge, but he only let his very best friends come up and play carrier-pigeon with him. But telling everyone had been a mistake. A group of older boys from down the block had a club—Aaron's mother called it a gang—and Aaron had longed to join as he had never longed for anything else. To be with them and share their secrets, the secrets of older boys. To be able to enter their clubhouse shack on the empty lot on the next street. To know the password and swear the secret oath. To belong.

About a month after Aaron had brought the pigeon home, Carl, the gang leader, walked over to Aaron in the street and told him he could be a member if he'd bring the pigeon down to be the club mascot. Aaron couldn't believe it; he immediately raced home to get Pidge. But his mother told Aaron to stay away from those boys, or else. And Aaron, miserable, argued with his mother and pleaded and cried and coaxed. It was no use. Not with those boys. No.

Aaron's mother tried to change the subject. She told him that it would soon be his grandmother's sixtieth birthday, a very special birthday indeed, and all the family from Brooklyn and the East Side would be coming to their apartment for a dinner and celebration. Would Aaron try to build something or make something for Grandma? A present made with his own hands would be nice. A decorated box for her hairpins or a crayon picture for her room or anything he liked.

In a flash Aaron knew what to give her: Pidge! Pidge would be her present! Pidge with his wing healed, who might be able to carry messages for her to the doctor or his Aunt Rachel or other people his grandmother seemed to go to a lot. It would be a surprise for everyone. And Pidge would make up for what had happened to Grandma when she'd been a little girl in the Ukraine, wherever that was.

Often, in the evening, Aaron's grandmother would talk about the old days long ago in the Ukraine, in the same way that she talked to the birds on the back fire escape. She had lived in a village near a place called Kishinev with hundreds of other poor peasant families like her own. Things hadn't been too bad under someone called Czar Alexander the Second, whom Aaron always pictured as a tall handsome man in a gold uniform. But Alexander the Second was assassinated, and Alexander the Third, whom Aaron pictured as an ugly man in a black cape, became the Czar. And the Jewish people of the Ukraine had no peace anymore.

One day, a thundering of horses was heard coming toward the village from the direction of Kishinev. *The Cossacks! The Cossacks!* someone had shouted. The Czar's horsemen! Quickly, quickly, everyone in Aaron's grandmother's family had climbed down to the cellar through a little trapdoor hidden under a mat in the big central room of their shack. But his grandmother's pet goat, whom she'd loved as much as Aaron loved Pidge and more, had to be left above, because if it had made a sound in the cellar, they would never have lived to see the next morning. They all hid under the wood in the woodbin and waited, hardly breathing.

Suddenly, from above, they heard shouts and calls and screams at a distance. And then the noise was in their house. Boots pounding on the floor, and everything breaking and crashing overhead. The smell of smoke and the shouts of a dozen men.

The terror went on for an hour and then the sound of horses' hooves faded into the distance. They waited another hour to make sure, and then the father went up out of the cellar and the rest of the family followed. The door to the house had been torn from its hinges and every piece of furniture was broken. Every window, every dish, every stitch of clothing was totally destroyed, and one wall had been completely bashed in. And on the floor was the goat, lying quietly. Aaron's grandmother, who was just a little girl of eight at the time, had wept over the goat all day and all night and could not be consoled.

But they had been lucky. For other houses had been burned to the ground. And everywhere, not goats alone, nor sheep, but men and women and children lay quietly on the ground. The word for this sort of massacre, Aaron had learned, was *pogrom*. It had been a pogrom. And the men on the horses were Cossacks. Hated word. Cossacks.

And so Pidge would replace that goat of long ago. A pigeon on Second Avenue where no one needed trapdoors or secret escape passages or woodpiles to hide under. A pigeon for his grandmother's sixtieth birthday. *Oh wing, heal quickly so my grandmother can send you flying to everywhere she wants!*

92

But a few days later, Aaron met Carl in the street again. And Carl told Aaron that there was going to be a meeting that afternoon in which a map was going to be drawn up to show where a secret treasure lay buried on the empty lot. "Bring the pigeon and you can come into the shack. We got a badge for you. A new kinda membership badge with a secret code on the back."

Aaron ran home, his heart pounding almost as fast as the pigeon's. He took Pidge in his hands and carried him out the door while his mother was busy in the kitchen making stuffed cabbage, his father's favorite dish. And by the time he reached the street, Aaron had decided to take the bandages off. Pidge would look like a real pigeon again, and none of the older boys would laugh or call him a bundle of rags.

Gently, gently he removed the bandages and the splints and put them in his pocket in case he should need them again. But Pidge seemed to hold his wing properly in place.

When he reached the empty lot, Aaron walked up to the shack, then hesitated. Four bigger boys were there. After a moment, Carl came out and commanded Aaron to hand Pidge over.

"Be careful," said Aaron. "I just took the bandages off."

"Oh sure, don't worry," said Carl. By now Pidge was used to people holding him, and he remained calm in Carl's hands.

"OK," said Carl. "Give him the badge." And one of the older boys handed Aaron his badge with the code on the back. "Now light the fire," said Carl.

"What . . . what fire?" asked Aaron.

"The fire. You'll see," Carl answered.

"You didn't say nothing about a fire," said Aaron. "You didn't say nothing to—"

"Hey!" said Carl. "I'm the leader here. And you don't talk unless I tell you that you have p'mission. Light the fire, Al."

The boy named Al went out to the side of the shack, where some wood and cardboard and old newspapers had been piled into a huge mound. He struck a match and held it to the newspapers.

"OK," said Carl. "Let's get 'er good and hot. Blow on it. Everybody blow."

Aaron's eyes stung from the smoke, but he blew alongside the others, going from side to side as the smoke shifted toward them and away.

"Let's fan it," said Al.

In a few minutes, the fire was crackling and glowing with a bright yellow-orange flame.

"Get me the rope," said Carl.

94

One of the boys brought Carl some cord and Carl, without a word, wound it twice around the pigeon, so that its wings were tight against its body.

"What . . . what are you *doing*!" shouted Aaron. "You're hurting his wing!"

"Don't worry about his wing," said Carl. "We're gonna throw him into the fire. And when we do, we're gonna swear an oath of loyalty to—"

"No! *No!*" shouted Aaron, moving toward Carl.

"Grab him!" called Carl. "Don't let him get the pigeon!"

But Aaron had leaped right across the fire at Carl, taking him completely by surprise. He threw Carl back against the shack and hit out at his face with both fists. Carl slid down to the ground and the pigeon rolled out of his hands. Aaron scooped up the pigeon and ran, pretending he was on roller skates so that he would go faster and faster. And as he ran across the lot he pulled the cord off Pidge and tried to find a place, *any* place, to hide him. But the boys were on top of him, and the pigeon slipped from Aaron's hands.

"Get him!" shouted Carl.

Aaron thought of the worst, the most horrible thing he could shout at the boys. "Cossacks!" he screamed. "You're all Cossacks!"

Two boys held Aaron back while the others tried

to catch the pigeon. Pidge fluttered along the ground just out of reach, skittering one way and then the other. Then the boys came at him from two directions. But suddenly Pidge beat his wings in rhythm, and rose up, up, over the roof of the nearest tenement, up over Second Avenue toward the park.

With the pigeon gone, the boys turned toward Aaron and tackled him to the ground and punched him and tore his clothes and punched him some more. Aaron twisted and turned and kicked and punched back, shouting "Cossacks! Cossacks!" And somehow the word gave him the strength to tear away from them.

When Aaron reached home, he tried to go past the kitchen quickly so his mother wouldn't see his bloody face and torn clothing. But it was no use; his father was home from work early that night and was seated in the living room. In a moment Aaron was surrounded by his mother, father, and grandmother, and in another moment he had told them everything that had happened, the words tumbling out between his broken sobs. Told them of the present he had planned, of the pigeon for a goat, of the gang, of the badge with the secret code on the back, of the shack, and the fire, and the pigeon's flight over the tenement roof.

And Aaron's grandmother kissed him and thanked him for his present which was even better than the pigeon.

"What present?" asked Aaron, trying to stop the series of sobs.

And his grandmother opened her pocketbook and handed Aaron her mirror and asked him to look. But all Aaron saw was his dirty, bruised face and his torn shirt.

Aaron thought he understood and then, again, he thought he didn't. How could she be so happy when there really was no present? And why pretend that there was?

Later that night, just before he fell asleep, Aaron tried to imagine what his grandmother might have done with the pigeon. She would have fed it, and she certainly would have talked to it, as she did to all the birds, and . . . and then she would have let it go free. Yes, of course. Pidge's flight to freedom must have been the gift that had made his grandmother so happy. Her goat has escaped from the Cossacks at last, Aaron thought, half dreaming. And he fell asleep with a smile.

The Hanukkah Santa Claus

ONCE, when the streets of New York rang with the cries of peddlers selling their goods, there lived a very poor, a very old, a very kind peddler from Moscow named Samuel Moscowitz. He lived alone in the poorest of the poor part of the city.

As a child in Moscow, he had never had any toys, except for the few his father had made from sticks and string. And so, in America, Samuel had decided to sell toys instead of vegetables or fish or scarves or umbrellas or the thousand other goods that peddlers sold.

Every day, Samuel went out pushing his big green cart filled with toys. Not the toys you have today but the toys of yesterday. Dolls stuffed with straw, which

Samuel called *kishkes*. And wooden wagons big enough to hold a toy army. And heavy iron fire engines pulled by heavy iron horses. And banks shaped like millionaires with coin slots in their top hats, which Samuel called *loch-in-kopfs*. And balls and balloons and four-sided tops called *dreidels*.

The children who lived near Second Avenue would walk alongside Samuel's cart as he pushed it through the streets. They came whenever he had new toys, and especially before Christmas or Hanukkah, the Feast of Lights, which usually fell close to Christmas. How long, how hungrily they looked. Ah, if only Samuel didn't have to take money when he sold the loch-in-kopfs and kishkes and dreidels. But Samuel had to live, and to live he had to pay for food and rent and, indeed, for more toys to sell. Still it troubled him deeply. Why couldn't toys grow like apples, and drop to the ground each autumn?

But afterward, when they finally tired of looking at the toys, the children would follow Samuel at a distance, like detectives, to see if they could find out where he lived. In those days, children were very good at trailing peddlers to their hideouts and secret caverns and other mysterious places.

But Samuel was always on the alert. Up Second Avenue, across Fourth Street, down Third Avenue and around and up went Samuel with his green push-cart full of kishkes and loch-in-kopfs. He never went home until late at night when the children were almost asleep. And he always left early in the morning before they awoke. No one guessed that he really lived on the same block as the children, in a little room tucked away at the top of a tenement, high above the elevated trains that squealed and grumbled by. But he knew he must never let the children find out where he lived, because then the game would be over. None of the other peddlers understood this, but Samuel understood because he had been a child once in Moscow—many oceans, rivers, and worlds away.

So naturally enough, the children all decided that Samuel lived at the North Pole. And one little boy asked very bravely whether Mr. Moscowitz came from the North Pole. Samuel shook his head and pointed toward Elias Katz, the curtain-and-tablecloth man, and said, "Pole." Then he pointed to himself and said, "Russian." But the children knew it was just a false clue to throw them off the track.

Then one little girl said, "He must be Santa Claus because he's old and he's fat and has sort of a grayish beard, and he lives at the North Pole." And another girl said, "He can't be. We don't ever have Santa Claus for Hanukkah. Do you?"

The children decided to ask Samuel Moscowitz if he was just possibly Santa Claus, in a very, very clever disguise. Samuel Moscowitz listened to the question with both thumbs tucked under his suspenders, as learned men sometimes do in the synagogue.

Then Samuel smiled a learned man's smile, which can be a very great smile indeed. And the children knew they had discovered his secret. They started to clap and jump as detectives do when they solve a case. "He's Santa Claus! He's Santa Claus!" they shouted. And Samuel smiled and pushed his pushcart toward Third Avenue.

That night, the first night of Hanukkah, Samuel Moscowitz lay awake on his mattress on the floor, looking up at the stars through his open window. Samuel could see everything quite clearly, because his window had no curtains at the moment. The curtains were being mended by Rachel Katz, the curtain-and-tablecloth man's wife.

As Samuel watched the stars in the clear December sky they seemed to bounce like beads before his eyes. They shivered and flashed above the tenement roofs across the street like spangles that had fallen off one of his little toy purses.

Then he sighed a very Russian sigh which went something like this: *Ah ah haha humm kremph.*

Samuel Moscowitz was troubled, and because he was troubled he sighed again and again. He had smiled at the children instead of telling the truth, and it was as if he had told a lie. And when the holiday toys didn't appear like magic, when the children saw that he really wasn't Santa Claus, would they ever walk beside his cart again, or trail him like detectives?

Maybe God would forgive him. He looked up at the stars and watched while he sighed: *Ah ah haha humm kremph*. But God did not reply. Even the stars stopped bouncing.

Samuel sighed again. He knew God rarely replied directly since God was, in fact, very elusive. Samuel had tried to find God's hideouts and secret caverns and other mysterious places all his life, but he always fell asleep too soon.

So he stopped watching the stars and lowered his sight to the tenement windows across the street. The windows looked warm and good in the night, like pieces of buttered toast that had just popped out of the fire escapes. But to Samuel they weren't just windows. They were all the children who followed him in the streets, and their brothers and sisters and mothers and fathers as well.

He loved to watch them moving about, like mario-nettes in tiny theatres. The shades went up or down like curtains. The lights went on and new stories began; the lights went off and old stories ended. And Samuel applauded within himself.

Then he fell asleep and dreamed about Moscow and oceans and fields and faces. And sometimes, in his sleep, he laughed a little, and sometimes he cried a little, and sometimes he just went *ah ah haha humm kremph.*

Then he dreamed about the windows across the street. Someone was lighting a *menorah*, a candle holder, for Hanukkah. There were children watching, counting as each candle in the menorah was lit in turn. The fire escapes, the windows, the menorah. His dream made him dizzy. So much light. So many people moving—red, green, blue, yellow—in their Russian peasant clothes. His mother was there. And someone had just given him a little bag of *kopecks*, pennies for toys—the toys he had never had as a child.

Then Samuel woke up with a start and sat up stiff and straight because he had an idea, and he knew it wasn't really *his* idea but his *dream's* idea. And he was frightened a little because his dreams always had better ideas than he did. How could that be?

Samuel dressed in the dark. Then he went down two flights to Elias Katz's apartment and knocked and waited and knocked and waited and knocked and the door opened. Samuel told Elias that he wanted to buy a very large curtain, used, or else a medium-sized tablecloth, also used. Hurry!

Elias yawned and told Samuel that he must have been celebrating Hanukkah with *schnapps* and was drunk and should go back upstairs to sleep. Samuel tapped Elias on the shoulder very seriously, as one must do at times, and asked for his own curtains back, repaired or not repaired. Elias yawned and went inside to get the curtains, then returned and yawned some more. *"Ah ooo hum ha,"* yawned Elias. *"Ah ah haha humm kremph,"* sighed Samuel.

Then Samuel rushed down to the little room in the basement where he kept his green pushcart and spread the curtains on the cement floor. Quickly he filled the curtains with kishkes and loch-in-kopfs and balls and balloons and dreidels. Then he tied all the toys together in the two curtains. With a bundle thrown over each shoulder, he hurried outdoors to the dark, sad night of Second Avenue.

It was late, much too late for people to be out in December, too late for any sensible policeman to be out, or even for a dog or a cat or a bird. Only Samuel Moscowitz was out that December night.

He stopped beneath the fire escape of the tenement across the street and put down his bundles. Then

Samuel tried to reach the movable iron ladder above his head. It was too high. You could lower it from above if you were escaping from a fire, but you couldn't reach it from below. They were made that way to keep robbers and Samuel Moscowitz from climbing up.

So Samuel threw the two bundles over both shoulders again and went inside the building. Slowly, with many, many *ah-ah-haha-humm-kremph*s, Samuel climbed the old shaky stairs to the second floor, to the third floor, to the fourth.

At last he reached the top floor and the narrow flight of steps that led to the roof. Up went Samuel, the curtains loaded with toys swaying dangerously behind him, up to the little door that opened out onto the roof. He stood there a moment. His white breath in the cold, clean air swirled round his shoulders like a *talis,* a shawl worn during prayers. The stars were all about him and above him, as bright as they had been long ago above the roofs and fields of Russia. And it made him want to sing. So he did. To the new stars above America, he sang a little song about the old stars above Russia.

Then he went to the edge of the roof, at the rear of the building where the uppermost ladder of a fire escape hung down. He swung around and over the roof ledge, down onto the ladder, holding his bundles with one hand as best he could. One step, two steps, three. He paused. Then a fourth step, a fifth. Suddenly his foot slipped. The stars swirled above him as his hand slid and he let go and . . .

He floated slowly out and away from the brick building, floated down to the level of the topmost window, paused there a moment, then gently, gently opened the window and floated through.

Red, green, blue, yellow, the candles in the menorah burned. Samuel blew on them very softly and watched the flames bend and dance and become a circus—a tame bear waltzing, a lady on a horse, acrobats leaping through hoops, red, green, blue, yellow.

Then he reached into his curtain-sack and pulled out a kishke and a loch-in-kopf and put them next to the menorah. And he put pennies in the slot in the top hat for good luck and pennies in the pocket of the dress of the doll stuffed with straw. Then he floated out to the next window.

And to the next, and the next, all night long. So many toys, like waves in the ocean he had crossed long ago, like grass in the fields of Russia, toys and toys and toys. Little sleighs with bells and wooden horses, little cups and samovars, toy whistles and

toy swords. And kopecks hidden under lids, in cracks and crannies. And hard candy, and sugar, and dreidels.

Red, green, blue, yellow, the candles in the menorahs burned all night while the curtain-sacks grew lighter and lighter and all the tenement rooms filled with toys and toys and toys. Lighter the curtains, lighter, rippling in the breeze that blew fresh toward the east, toward the ocean.

And Samuel Moscowitz floated up, up, his empty curtains held out like sails, floated high above the roofs of the tenements of Second Avenue, above the poorest of the poor part of New York.

Higher, higher, Samuel flew, a great gliding bird with two white wings. Flew above all the sleeping people and all the avenues and all the tall buildings and all the short buildings of New York, toward the harbor. Out over the Atlantic above the churning, heaving, twisting sea; above the groaning ships bringing others to America; above the lights of lonely houses on the coast of Ireland; above the smoke and steam of busy London; across the fields and towns of France; the forests and rivers of Germany; onward and onward and onward Samuel flew.

Until the breeze fell to a murmur of voices, and the great wings softly let him down; down to the very edge of Moscow, to the very street, to the very house, to the very room, to the very bed that was waiting for him. The curtains fell over him like warm blankets; the murmur of voices fell over him like the voices of his mother and his father. And he slept and sighed *ah ah haha humm kremph,* but very gently, very, very gently.

And the children of Second Avenue in New York City never saw Samuel Moscowitz from Moscow again.

About the author

Myron Levoy was born in New York City. He received a master's degree in Chemical Engineering from Purdue University, and has worked as an engineer on nuclear propulsion projects for rockets and space vehicles. He and his wife and two children live in Rockaway, New Jersey.

Mr. Levoy has written adult novels, plays, and short stories, and his poems have appeared in magazines throughout the country. THE WITCH OF FOURTH STREET AND OTHER STORIES is his first book for young readers.

About the artist

Gabriel Lisowski was born in Jerusalem and grew up in Warsaw, Poland, and Vienna, Austria. He studied architecture in Vienna, but later switched to graphic design and illustration. Mr. Lisowski has worked in advertising art and has done children's posters and books. This is his first book for American readers.

Format by Kohar Alexanian
Set in 14 point Bodoni Book
Composed and bound by American Book–Stratford Press, Inc.
Printed by Halliday Lithograph Corp.
HARPER & ROW, PUBLISHERS, INC.